D0912934

To Elliadora, Luke, and Owen.

Amicus Illustrated is published by Amicus Learning, an imprint of Amicus
P.O. Box 227   Mankato, MN 56002   www.amicuspublishing.us

Library edition published in 2024 by Amicus. All rights reserved. No part of this book
may be reproduced in any form without written permission from the publisher.

This library-bound edition is reprinted by arrangement with Chronicle Books, LLC.

First published in the United States in 2022 by Chronicle Books, LLC.

Copyright © 2022 by Sergio Ruzzier.

Library of Congress Cataloging-in-Publication Data
Names: Ruzzier, Sergio, 1966- author, illustrator.
Title: Up and down and other stories.
Description: Library edition. Mankato, MN : Amicus Learning, 2024.
Series: Sergio Ruzzier's Fox & Chick First published in the United States
in 2022 by Chronicle Books, LLC. Audience: Ages 5-8. Audience: Grades K-1.
Summary: In three brief episodes about two unlikely friends, Fox talks Chick
down from the tree he has climbed, the two go sledding once they have
enough snowflakes, and Chick builds a bookcase.
Identifiers: LCCN 2023026213 ISBN 9781645498223 library binding
Subjects: CYAC: Graphic novels. Foxes--Fiction. Chickens--Fiction.
Friendship--Fiction. Humorous stories. LCGFT: Humorous fiction.
Funny animal comics. Graphic novels.
Classification: LCC PZ7.7.R94 Up 2024 DDC 741.5/973--dc23/eng/20230628
LC record available at https://lccn.loc.gov/2023026213"

Printed in China.

Design by Sara Gillingham Studio.
Handlettering by Sergio Ruzzier.
The illustrations in this book were rendered in pen, ink, and watercolor.

UP AND DOWN

and Other Stories

amicus
LEARNING

CONTENTS

UP AND
DOWN

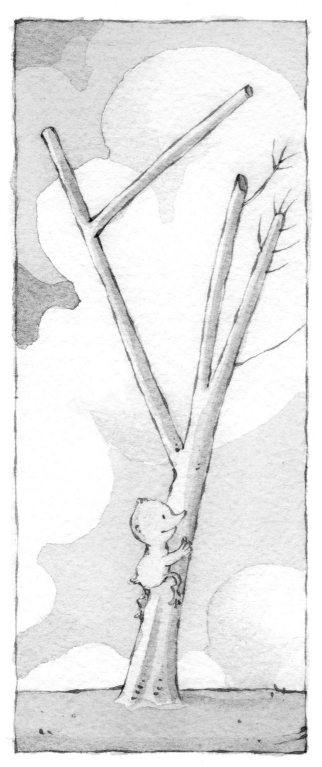
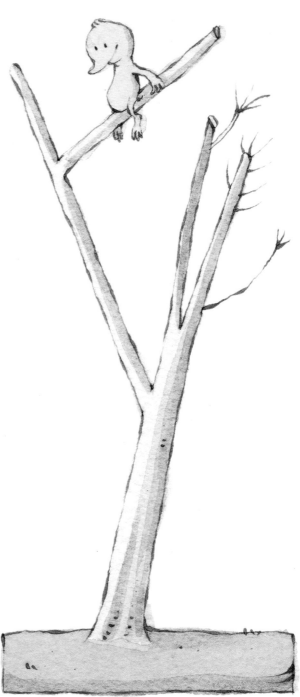

Are you
as good at
climbing
down a tree?

. . .

Oh, dear.

Fox, I will never be able to come down again!

I will go and get a ladder.

Please don't leave me alone!

But Chick, you can't stay there forever!

It's okay, Fox. I'll be up here forever, and you'll be down there forever.

You will bring me potato chips and chocolate cake.

You will tell me stories.

We will be fine.

It's getting dark, Chick.

If you are
here with me,
I will not be
afraid.

Climb down
the tree,
Chick. I know
you can do it.

It's not
too bad
up here
after all.

. . .

Chick, can
I ask you a
question?

12

Of course, Fox.

Can you show me how you climbed up the tree?

Sure.
Just a
moment.

Let me show you.

What I did was . . .

SEVENTEEN SNOWFLAKES

SEVENTEEN SNOWFLAKES

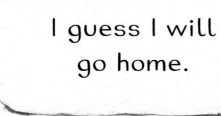

I guess I will
go home.

Wait!

21

Fox! It's snowing!
Let's sled!

Look!

Aww . . .

I'm sorry, Chick. But you need more than one snowflake to be able to go sledding.

No problem, Fox. I will go and wait for more snowflakes.

One, two,
three,
four . . .

five!

I counted five snowflakes!
Let's go sledding!

Chick, five snowflakes are not enough.

How many snowflakes do we need?

I don't know. I guess we would need at least one million snowflakes.

One million?! Whew.

Fox, the snowflakes are falling faster and faster. I could not count beyond seventeen.

Chick, if you cannot count all the snowflakes, we might have enough snow to go sledding!

Now we know, Fox:
We need at least
seventeen snowflakes!

THE NEW BOOKCASE

Chocolate cake is my favorite, but if it's a large meringue cake I will still eat it, Fox.

It's not a cake, Chick.

I see.

Is it four bags of potato chips?

If it's four bags of potato chips, I have to remember to drink some water.

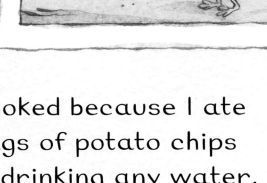

Once, I almost choked because I ate four bags of potato chips without drinking any water.

It's not potato chips, Chick.

Huh.

I can't think of anything else.

Here it is, Chick.

Huh.

It's a book,
Chick.

I know, but . . .

You don't like books, Chick?

It's not that I don't like books, Fox. But this is the first book that I have ever owned, and I don't know where to put it.

You can build a bookcase, Chick!

Good idea, Fox! I will
build one right now.

40

BANG!
BANG!
BANG!

Would you like to see my new bookcase, Fox?

I would
love to,
Chick.

It's a very nice bookcase, Chick. But what if you get more books?

You are right, Fox.

I will build a bigger new bookcase.

BANG!
BANG!
BANG!
BANG!
BANG!

Would you like to see my bigger new bookcase, Fox?

I would love to, Chick.